S0-AXO-794

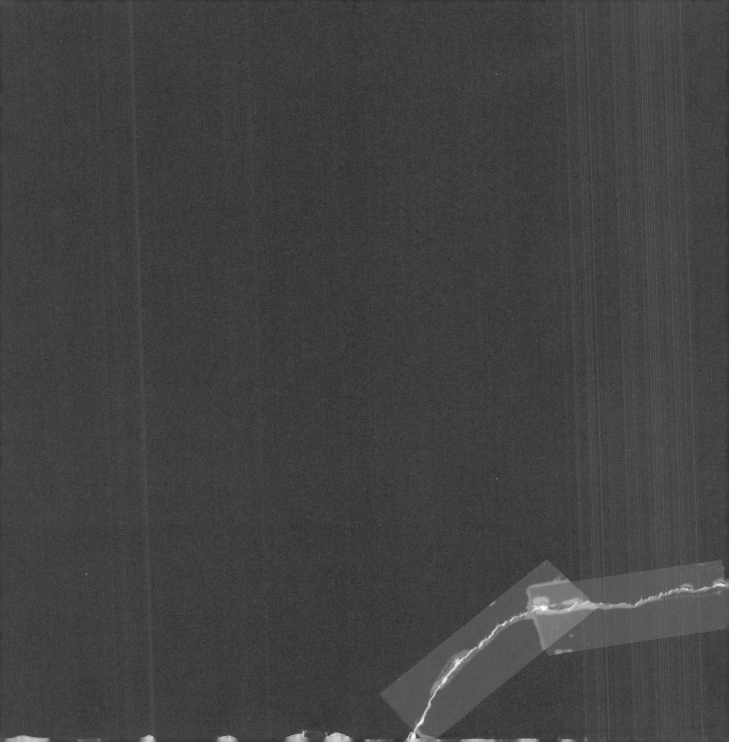

BABAR

and the Scary Day

Harry N. Abrams, Inc., Publishers

One day, Isabelle was in Babar's studio, drawing pictures. All of a sudden she heard a noise.

It was coming from above—from the attic. THUMP! it went. THUMP! THUMP!

Isabelle ran next door to the children's bedroom.

"Pom! Pom!" she yelled. "There's a scary monster in the attic! It's green, and it's huge!"

"Isabelle, stop imagining things," said Pom. "There's no monster in the attic."

But just then, there was another loud noise. THUMP-drag, it went. THUMP-drag.

"Eeeek!" screamed Pom and Isabelle.

The two of them ran down the hall to the playroom.

"Flora!" Isabelle yelled. "There's a monster in the attic! It's green, and it's huge!"

"It's dragging one foot!" added Pom.

"Don't be silly," said Flora. "There's no such thing as a huge, green, foot-dragging monster."

Just then, another noise came from the attic
staircase down the hall. THUMP-drag-rattle, it went.
THUMP-drag-rattle.

"Eeeek!" screamed Pom, Isabelle, and Flora.

The three of them ran down the stairs at the other end of the hall to the kitchen, where Alexander was having a snack.

"Alexander!" yelled Isabelle. "There's a monster coming to get us! It's green, and it's huge!"

"And it's dragging one foot!" said Pom.

"And it's rattling chains!" said Flora.

"Wait a second," said Alexander. "There's no such thing as a huge, green, foot-dragging, chain-rattling monster."

But just then, a noise came down the stairs toward the kitchen. THUMP-drag-rattle-clank, it went. THUMP-drag-rattle-clank.

"Eeeeeeek!" screamed Isabelle, Pom, Flora, and Alexander.

The four of them scrambled into the pantry. They huddled against the door, listening. THUMP-drag-rattle-clank, went the noise from upstairs. THUMP-drag-rattle-clank.

"I definitely think I saw it," whispered Alexander. "It's green. And it had a big bunch of dungeon keys it was clanking."

"What if it comes down here?" asked Flora.

After a few minutes, they realized that the noise had stopped.

"Do you think it's gone?" asked Isabelle.

"Don't know," said Pom, with a shudder.

A few more minutes went by. Finally, they decided to open the pantry door, very carefully.

Nobody was in the kitchen. The house was quiet.

"Look!" said Isabelle, pointing out the window.

Out in front of the palace was Babar. He was piling
tied-up bundles of newspapers and magazines, bags of
cans, and sacks of bottles at the curb.

THUMP, went the newspapers as he dropped them on the ground. Drag, went the bundles of magazines as he moved them onto the pile. Rattle, went the bags of cans. Clank, went the bottles.

"It's recycling day!" Babar announced to the children.
"Zephir and I just went through the whole palace,
collecting things for recycling. Whew—it's a monster of
a job!"

"We know!" said Isabelle, Pom, Flora, and Alexander.

Designer: Vivian Cheng
Production Manager: Jonathan Lopes

Library of Congress Cataloging-in-Publication Data

Weiss, Ellen, 1949–
Babar and the scary day / [text written by Ellen Weiss ; images adapted by Jean-Claude Gibert, after characters
created by Jean and Laurent de Brunhoff].
p. cm.
Summary: One after another the children become frightened as they hear strange noises coming from the attic
and imagine there is a horrible monster in the castle.
ISBN 0-8109-5019-7 (alk. paper)
[1. Noise—Fiction. 2. Fear—Fiction. 3. Elephants—Fiction. 4. Kings, queens, rulers, etc.—Fiction.] I. Gibert, Jean-
Claude, ill. II. Brunhoff, Jean de, 1899–1937. III. Brunhoff, Laurent de, 1925– IV. Title.

PZ7.W4475Bab 2004
[E]—dc22
2004000229

Printed and bound in China
10 9 8 7 6 5 4 3 2 1

Harry N. Abrams, Inc.
100 Fifth Avenue, New York, NY 10011
www.abramsbooks.com

Abrams is a subsidiary of

LA MARTINIÈRE